THIS BOOK BELONGS TO

_____

_____

The shape-shifting kelpie, or water horse,
was believed to live in many Scottish lochs and rivers,
especially in northern Scotland.
This story brings together elements of kelpie lore
from a variety of Scottish traditional tales,
including stories found in:
F. Marian McNeill, *The Silver Bough*, Vol. 1;
Otta Swire, *The Highlands and Their Legends*;
Jennifer Westwood and Sophia Kingshill,
The Lore of Scotland.

THE SECRET OF THE KELPIE

RETOLD BY
LARI DON

ILLUSTRATED BY
PHILIP LONGSON

Every loch in Scotland, however beautiful, has its dark cold depths.
And every loch in Scotland has its kelpie.
But it's easy to forget those dangers on a sunny afternoon.

One sunny Sunday, after lunch, the blacksmith's children decided to play hide and seek by the loch near their village.

The oldest brother, Fergus, strode ahead to carve his initials on a tall grey stone.

The youngest sister, Flora, covered her eyes and counted, "…ninety-nine, a hundred, coming ready or not!"

But Flora didn't find her sisters and brothers. Instead she found…

"A horse! I found a beautiful white horse!"

Her sisters and brothers rushed out of their hiding places to look. The most perfect horse they'd ever seen turned towards them and snickered softly.

"Who does it belong to?" asked Flora.

"It can't be from a farm," said Fergus, "not with that fancy saddle."

"Maybe it's a pretty princess's horse," said Agnes.

"Maybe it's a brave knight's horse," said Archie.

Fergus looked round. "Its owner isn't here right now. Who wants a quick shottie?"

"I do! I do!" All the children put their hands up. All except Flora, who was looking at wet hoofprints on the dry ground.

"Two at a time!" Fergus lifted Mhairi then Magnus onto the gleaming horse's back. "There's room for more. This horse is bigger than I thought!"

He lifted Agnes up.

"There's still space! You can all go for a ride!" Fergus lifted Archie up. "What about you, wee one?"

"No thanks," said Flora.

"Plenty of room for me, then!"

As Fergus climbed up, Flora frowned. "I think that horse is getting bigger, so you can all fit on."

"Don't be daft," said Fergus. "Come and have fun with the rest of us."

Flora shook her head.

"I think that horse came out of the loch," said Flora. "I think you should all get off!"

The horse started to walk towards the loch.

"No, nice horsie, not that way," said Fergus. "Let's go up into the fields." He grabbed the mane to guide its head away from the water. The horse ignored him and kept walking towards the loch.

"I can't turn it!"

"Jump off!" shouted Flora.

Her brothers and sisters yelled:

"We can't jump off!"

"We can't get down!"

"We can't move!"

"We're all *stuck*!"

Flora gasped. "I know what that horse is!"

"It's a *kelpie*!" she shouted. "Remember the old stories? It's tricked you onto its back, now it's taking you into the loch to drown you and eat you!"

Fergus was still trying to turn the horse away from the loch, but his hands were tangled in its mane.

The other brothers and sisters wriggled and struggled, but they still couldn't get off. They all started to scream as the horse's hooves splashed into the shallow water.

"Don't panic!" called Flora. "Let me think!"

As Flora watched the horse carry her family steadily away, she took a deep breath and leant on the tall grey stone. "Let me think…" Her hand touched the old carvings.

She bent down. The biggest carving showed an animal rising out of the loch.

"Wait," she whispered. "I've found something…"

"A spade, an axe, a sword. They're all made of metal!"
She looked up. The kelpie didn't have an iron bit between
its teeth, or iron stirrups by its flanks, or iron horseshoes
on its hooves.

"That's the kelpie's secret weakness," she murmured.
"It can't stand metal!" Then she yelled as loud as she could:
"Do you have anything metal?"

"My penknife's in my boot," Fergus called back, "but my hands are caught in the mane!"

"I left my comb in the house!" shouted Mhairi.

Magnus yelled, "I've got the back-door key." He swung the key on its chain and hit the horse's flank.

The kelpie screamed and reared high in the air.

Magnus and Mhairi and Agnes and Archie all fell off.

But as the horse crashed back down, Fergus was still stuck, with his hands tangled in the mane.

The kelpie trotted towards the middle of the loch. Flora chased after it, hoping to cut her big brother free.

Fergus hauled back on the horse's head, slowing it down. Flora splashed through the water, trying to catch up. The kelpie waded deeper and deeper into the loch.

Flora reached the kelpie just as the water reached her waist. She stretched up and slid the knife out of her brother's boot, then jumped up and slashed at the kelpie's mane.

The horsehair sizzled when the iron blade touched it. Fergus ripped his hands free and fell into the water.

Flora hauled him spluttering to his feet and they backed away from the horse.

The beautiful horse began to change into something huge and ugly and hungry. Steam swirled from its nostrils, waves swirled round its hooves. Its head arched high above Flora and Fergus.

Fergus grabbed the knife from his sister and waved it at the kelpie. "We have a metal blade! You stay there. You leave us alone!"

The kelpie stood still as Flora and Fergus dragged each other towards the shore, where their brothers and sisters stood shivering and shaking. The kelpie watched Flora and Fergus struggle out of the water, then it sank into the dark cold depths of the loch.

Soon the children were safe at home, warming up and drying off.

"I knew there was something strange about that horse," said Agnes.

"No you didn't," said Archie. "You thought it was a pretty princess's horse."

"*You* thought it was a brave knight's horse!" laughed Agnes.

"Flora knew what it was," said Fergus. "She worked out the kelpie's secret and she saved us."

Flora smiled. "Let's make the carvings on the stone clearer, to warn the next family who play by the loch."

The kelpie stone is still there today: a warning to all the local children, and perhaps to you, never to trust a beautiful horse with wet hooves, and always to carry something metal in your pocket.